Acting Edition

The 39 Steps, Even More Abridged

Adapted by
Patrick Barlow

From the novel by
John Buchan

From the movie by Alfred Hitchcock

Licensed by ITV Global Entertainment Limited

And an original concept by Simon Corble
and Nobby Dimon

ISBN 978-0-573-70957-9

www.concordtheatricals.com
www.concordtheatricals.co.uk
Cover Illustration by Mark Thomas

MUSIC AND THIRD-PARTY MATERIALS USE NOTE

IMPORTANT BILLING AND CREDIT REQUIREMENTS

All producers of *The 39 Steps, Even More Abridged* must give credit to the Author of the Play in all programmes distributed in connection with performances of the Play, and in all instances in which the title of the Play appears for the purposes of advertising, publicizing or otherwise exploiting the Play and/or a production. The name of the Author must appear on a separate line on which no other name appears, immediately following the title and must appear in size of type not less than fifty per cent of the size of the title type.

In addition the following credit must be given in all programmes and publicity information distributed in association with this piece:

THE 39 STEPS, EVEN MORE ABRIDGED

Adapted by Patrick Barlow

From the novel by John Buchan

From the movie by Alfred Hitchcock,

licensed by ITV Global Entertainment Limited

And an original concept by Simon Corble and Nobby Dimon

FIREARMS AND OTHER WEAPONS USED IN THEATRE PRODUCTIONS

With regards to the rules and regulations of firearms and other weapons used in theatre productions, we recommend that you read the Entertainment Information Sheet No. 20 (Health and Safety Executive). This information sheet is one of a series produced in consultation with the Joint Advisory Committee for Broadcasting and the Performing Arts. It gives guidance on the management of weapons that are part of a production, including fi rearms, replicas and deactivated weapons.

This sheet may be downloaded from: www.hse.gov.uk.

CHARACTERS

RICHARD HANNAY
COMPERE
MR MEMORY
ANNABELLA SCHMIDT
BUSINESS MAN 1
BUSINESS MAN 2
POLICEMAN 1
POLICEMAN 2
PAMELA EDWARDS
LOUISA JORDAN
PROFESSOR JORDAN
SHERIFF
INSPECTOR
LITTLE VOICE
VOICES
DUNWOODY
MR MCQUARRIE
HEAVY 1
HEAVY 2
MRS MCGARRIGLE
MR MCGARRIGLE
SUPERINTENDANT ALBRIGHT

SETTING

London, Edinburgh and the Scottish Highlands

TIME

1935

AUTHOR'S NOTES

The 39 Steps, Even More Abridged is the 40-minute (approx) version of my play *The 39 Steps*.

It is written for four actors: three men and a woman.

HANNAY is played by one man throughout.

The woman plays **ANNABELLA** and **PAMELA**.

The other two actors we call the **TWO MEN** play all other parts. They can be played by two men, two women or a man and a woman.

NB It is possible (and I have seen it done) – to cast the play with a company of at least fifty. Rather more expensive but jolly good fun.

STYLE OF PLAYING

This is not a naturalistic play.

That should be born in mind throughout. It should be played in the rapid, clipped and heightened style of 1930s thrillers.

SPEED and CLARITY are of the essence.

There should be no pauses in the dialogue apart from when it says *PAUSE* ie those moments of the most essential *DRAMATIC* nature.

'*The Professor raises his little finger. 'Are you sure it wasn't – PAUSE – this one?!'*

This is essential.

Finally, the more the audience is several steps behind the better.

Do not wait for them.

They'll catch up.

They'll thank you for it.

HANNAY. *(Voice.)* What are the Thirty-Nine Steps? What are the Thirty-Nine Steps? *What are the Thirty-Nine –*

MUSIC: ["MR MEMORY THEME"]

(Lights up on:)

OVERTURE

(The company run on. Furiously pull on the set for Scene One. They bow and exit. [NB Perhaps funnier if it is just the **TWO MEN** *who do all scene-shifting].)*

Music Hall. Night.

MUSIC: ["MR MEMORY THEME"]

(**COMPERE** *and* **MR MEMORY** *enter. Bow.*)

(*Sound effects: Applause.*)

COMPERE.   Good evenin' ladies and gentlemen and welcome to tonight's performance. And to begin our show tonight, please welcome one of the most remarkable men in the whole world. The astounding and amazing Mr Memory!!!

(*Sound effects: Applause.*)

The man with a million facts at his fingertips. With more facts in his brain than is possible to conceive! Is there nothing he does not know? Come on folks – let's find out! Are you ready for the questions Mr Memory?

MR MEMORY. Quite ready for the questions, thankoo!

(*Sound effects: Applause.*)

MUSIC: ["DRUMROLL"]

COMPERE. So first question please ladies and gents.

(*Points round audience.*)

Beg pardon sir? What was that? Who won the Cup in 1926 Mr Memory?

MR MEMORY. Who won the Cup in 1926? The Tottenham Hotspurs won the Cup in 1926, defeating the Arsenal Gunners by five goals to nil. Am I right sir?

COMPERE. Quite right, Mr Memory!!

(*Sound effects: Applause.*)

COMPERE. Ah yes! Here's another!

(Points into audience.)

Thank you madam. What was Napoleon's 'orse called?

MR MEMORY. Napoleon's 'orse was called Bellerephon. What he rode at the Battle of Waterloo sufferin severely from the 'aemorroids on June 18th 1815. Am I right madam?

(Sound effects: Applause.)

COMPERE. Very good Mr Memory! And now ladies and –

(RICHARD HANNAY *appears in the box.)*

Ah! Here's a gentleman with a question. Your question sir please?

HANNAY. My what?

COMPERE. I'd say you was a military gentleman am I right sir?

HANNAY. Um – I was yes.

COMPERE. I thought that from your proud bearin sir. Good for you sir. Done his bit for king and country I should wager! A big round of applause please for the brave soldier ladies and gents!

(Sound effects: Applause.)

Who, with his brave comrades, set forth to make the world a better place. A new world! A better world! Give us 'ope for mankind and for the future!

HANNAY. Sadly not. Didn't make the world a better place. Didn't set forth to do anything! Did what I was told and didn't talk back. That's all. Nothing's changed.

The world as bad as it always was! Little hope in anything I'm afraid. Sorry to disappoint.

(Sound effects: Applause peters out.)

COMPERE. Ah well, ne'er mind sir! Have a nice night in the theatre why don't you? Might as well sir.

HANNAY. Might as well? Might as well just –

(*Mimes blowing brains out.*)

COMPERE. Oh come on sir! Chin up! How about a question for Mr Memory while you're 'ere sir?

HANNAY. I don't have a question for Mr Memory! Or Mr anybody! No questions left I'm afraid. Sorry. Goodnight.

(**HANNAY** *turns. Bumps straight into* **ANNABELLA SCHMIDT**, *elegant in black.*)

ANNABELLA. Excuse me.

HANNAY. Oh – um –

ANNABELLA. Is this seat taken?

HANNAY. Er –

ANNABELLA. Thank you.

(*She sits.* **HANNAY** *gazes transfixed.*)

COMPERE. Right. Another question please? Anything at all? Geographical? Historical? Scientifical?

ANNABELLA. (*Looks into audience.*) Sheisse!

(*She pulls out a gun. Fires.* **MR MEMORY** *and* **COMPERE** *go into shock.*)

(*Sound effects: Audience pandemonium.*)

Excuse me?

HANNAY. Yes?

ANNABELLA. May I come home with you?

HANNAY. What?

COMPERE. That was Mr Memory!

(Sound effects: Applause.)

ANNABELLA. *PLEASE! You have to!*

HANNAY. Well – um – it's a little tricky at the moment. I've got the – er – decorators in and um –

(She runs out. He follows.)

Well, it's your funeral!

COMPERE. Thank you Mr Memory.

(Applause.)

(Shoves him off. Shouts into pit.)

Play man, play!!

MUSIC: ["MR MEMORY THEME"]

Don't forget his name now!

MR MEMORY. *(Runs back.)* Mr Memory!

COMPERE. Quite right Mr Memory! Thankoo!

MR MEMORY. Thankoo!

*(**MR MEMORY** bows. **COMPERE** shoves him off. Bows. Exits.)*

(Applause/ Music: Ends.)

Hannay's Appartment. Night.

(A table with a phone, covered in a dust sheet. A window with a blind. **HANNAY** *and* **ANNABELLA** *enter. She opens the door, looks out, closes door.)*

ANNABELLA. Thank you Mr Hannay!

HANNAY. How do you know my name?

ANNABELLA. I saw it in the lobby. Richard Hannay. Portland Mansions, Portland Place.

HANNAY. Ah yes.

(Sound effects: Telephone rings.)

Hello there's the telephone.

ANNABELLA. *Don't answer it please!!!*

HANNAY. Why not?

ANNABELLA. Because I think it is for me.

*(**HANNAY** pulls off dust sheet, picks up phone. It keeps ringing. He slams it down. It rings again. He slams it down again. It stops. Awkward moment.)*

HANNAY. So – may I know your name?

ANNABELLA. You don't want to know my name. Schmidt. Annabella Schmidt.

HANNAY. Well Annabella Schmidt, you fired that shot in the theatre didn't you? It wasn't a great show but it wasn't that bad.

ANNABELLA. It was a diversion. There were two men in the theatre trying to shoot me.

HANNAY. Beautiful mysterious woman pursued by gunmen. Sounds like a spy story.

ANNABELLA. That's exactly what it is. Only I prefer the word "agent" better.

HANNAY. "Secret agent" I suppose? For which country?

ANNABELLA. I have no country.

HANNAY. Born in a balloon, eh?

ANNABELLA. Now listen very carefully Mr Hannay! I am being pursued by a very brilliant secret agent of a certain foreign power who is on the point of obtaining highly confidential information *VITAL* to your air defence. I tracked two of his men to that Music Hall. Unfortunately they recognised me. They are in the street this moment. Beneath your English lamp post.

> (**HANNAY** *lifts the blind.* **TWO MEN** *run on in trilbies and trench coats. They carry a street lamp. They pose beneath it in film noir mode. Run off again with the lamp.*)

Now do you believe me?

> (**HANNAY** *lifts blind to be sure. The men run on again with the lamp.*)

HANNAY. Alright. You win!

> (*The men run off with the lamp.*)

ANNABELLA. Mr Hannay, I am going to tell you something now which is not very healthy. It will mean either life. Or death. But if I tell you then you are – inwolved.

HANNAY. In what?

ANNABELLA. Inwolved.

> (**HANNAY** *lifts the blind. The* **TWO MEN,** *not expecting this, rush on again with the lamp.* **HANNAY** *turns.*)

HANNAY. Alright!! Tell me!!!

*(The men gasp exhaustedly. Run off again
with the lamp.)*

ANNABELLA. Have you heard of the Thirty-Nine Steps?

HANNAY. What's that, a pub?

ANNABELLA. Enough of your English humour Mr Hannay
please! All I can tell you is if these men are not stopped,
it is only of matter of days, perhaps hours before the top
secret and highly confidential information is out of the
country. And when they've got it out of the country –
God help us all! God help the world!!

HANNAY. The world!!?

ANNABELLA. Yes Richard! And now we are the only people
who can stop them! You don't know what they're like
my friend! How clever their chief is! He has a dozen
names! A hundred faces! He can look like a thousand
people! But one thing he cannot disguise. This part of
his little finger –

*(She lifts his little finger, links her little finger
into his little finger.)*

– is missing. So if ever you should meet a man with no
top joint here – be very careful my friend.

HANNAY. I'll remember that.

ANNABELLA. *(Gazing into his eyes.)* Richard?

HANNAY. *(Gazing into hers.)* Yes?

ANNABELLA. Do you –

HANNAY. Do I –

ANNABELLA. – have a map?

HANNAY. A map?

ANNABELLA. A map of Scotland.

HANNAY. Map of Scotland?

ANNABELLA. I just said that.

HANNAY. There's a detailed map of Scotland in my room. Under the section – "Scotland."

ANNABELLA. There is a man in Scotland I must visit if anything is to be done. An Englishman. Professor Jordan. He lives at a place called – Alt-na-Shell-achhhhh.

HANNAY. I beg your pardon?

ANNABELLA. Alt-na-Shell-achhhhhhhh!

HANNAY. Alt-na-Shell-achhhhhh!? And the Thirty-Nine –

ANNABELLA. Good night... Richard.

> *(She disappears into the darkness.* **HANNAY** *gazes after her entranced.)*

HANNAY. Goodnight... Annabella.

Hannay's Flat. An Hour Later.

["HAUNTING MUSIC"]*

(HANNAY *in the armchair, Trying to sleep.*
ANNABELLA *looms out of the shadows. The*
map in her hand.)

ANNABELLA. *(Huskily.)* Richard? Richard?

HANNAY. Annabella!! What are you doing!? Can't you
sleep? I can't either. I see you found the map. Did you
find – what's it called –

ANNABELLA.   Alt-na-shellachhhhhh!!   Alt-na-
shellachhhhhh!!

(*Cries out.*)

Aggghhh!

(*Collapses across him. A knife in her back.*
HANNAY *springs back.*)

HANNAY. *Annabella!!!*

ANNABELLA. He got me. The man with the little finger
missing. He'll get you next. His men will stop at
nothing! Quick Richard! Escape! And save the world!
To Scotland Richard! To Scotland!

(*She judders up and down with death throes.*
Dies on his lap. He looks up.)

HANNAY. Golly!

---

* A license to produce THE 39 STEPS, EVEN MORE ABRIDGED does
not include a performance license for any third-party or copyrighted
music. Licensees should create an original composition or use music in
the public domain. For further information, please see Music Use Note
on page 3.

(He wriggles awkwardly under her dead body. Wrenches the map from her hand. It is enormous. He wrestles with it, studying every inch. At last he finds what he is looking for:)

Alt na Shellach! *Alt na Shellachhhhh!!!!!*

(Sound effects: Distant front door opens.)

*(**HANNAY** freezes.)*

["DRAMATIC MUSIC"]*

*(Sound effects: Footsteps come upstairs. Closer and closer. Closer and closer. Closer and closer. **HANNAY** freezes)*

(Sound effects: Train whistle shrieks.)

Edinburgh Train. Compartment. Day.

VOICES. All aboard for the Highlands! All aboard for the Highlands!

> *(The company create the compartment with chairs. **HANNAY** leaps in. Exhausted. Hat over his eyes.)*

> *(Sound effects: Train noises.)*

> *(The train sets off. **HANNAY** rocks with the train. Two **BUSINESS MEN** appear. They jump in.)*

BUSINESS MAN 1. Just made it!

BUSINESS MAN 2. That was lucky!

BUSINESS MAN 1. Anyone sitting here?

HANNAY. Only me.

BUSINESS MAN 2. Mind if we do?

HANNAY. Not at all.

BUSINESS MAN 1. Thanks very much. Excuse me.

> *(They squeeze past.)*

Sorry. Sorry.

BUSINESS MAN 2. Sorry. Sorry.

HANNAY. Sorry.

> *(They squeeze past him and sit. They all start to rock with the train.)*

BUSINESS MAN 1. Lovely day.

HANNAY. Lovely yes.

BUSINESS MAN 2. Here look at this.

(He pulls out a newspaper. Reads out.)

"Woman murdered in a fashionable West End flat! Portland Mansions. Portland Place".

*(**HANNAY** freezes.)*

BUSINESS MAN 1. Go on go on.

BUSINESS MAN 2. "Well-dressed woman about thirty-five with a knife in her back. The tenant – Richard Hannay – is missing". Terrible.

BUSINESS MAN 1. Terrible!

*(They look at **HANNAY**.)*

HANNAY. Terrible!

BUSINESS MAN 2. "Approximately thirty-seven. Wavy hair. Light brown eyes. Pencil moustache."

*(**HANNAY** lowers his hat, hides his moustache.)*

BUSINESS MAN 1. Think I'll pop out to the buffet car. Fancy anythin? Biscuit? Sandwich? Nice bit of cake?

BUSINESS MAN 2. No thank you.

HANNAY. No thank you.

*(**BUSINESS MAN 1** squeezes out.)*

BUSINESS MAN 1. Sorry. Sorry.

BUSINESS MAN 2. Sorry. Sorry.

HANNAY. Sorry.

(Sound effects: Train shrieks.)

*(**BUSINESS MAN 1** exits. Comes running back.)*

BUSINESS MAN 1. 'Ere guess what?

BUSINESS MAN 2. What?

BUSINESS MAN 1. The train's full of police!

(*HANNAY freezes with shock.*)

BUSINESS MAN 2. Police!!!???

BUSINESS MAN 1. Wosser problem? Got somethin to hide?

BUSINESS MAN 2. Course not!

BUSINESS MAN 1. We're in the clear anyway.

(*They all laugh.* **HANNAY** *jumps up.*)

HANNAY. Sorry – um – just going to the er – lavatory. Excuse me.

(*Squeezes out.*)

Sorry. Sorry.

BUSINESS MEN. Sorry. Sorry.

HANNAY. Sorry.

(**HANNAY** *exits.*)

BUSINESS MAN 2. Too much 'aggis probably.

BUSINESS MAN 1. Probably!

(*They both laugh.*)

(*Sound effects: Train piercing whistle. Train roars into tunnel.*)

Highland Train. Corridor. Night.

(Lights flash. Train rattles. **HANNAY** *lurches down the corridor. He stops! Stares in front of him.)*

POLICEMAN 1. *(Voice over.)* Excuse me please. Sorry to disturb ye. Have ye seen this man? His name is Richard Hannay.

*(***HANNAY*** *turns. Heads back in the other direction. Stops! Stares in front of him.)*

POLICEMAN 2. *(Voice over.)* Excuse me please. Sorry to disturb ye. Have ye seen this man? His name is Richard Hannay.

*(***HANNAY*** *is trapped! The* **POLICEMEN** *getting closer. He looks into the next compartment.)*

(Lights up on:)

Highland Train. Pamela's Compartment. Night.

(**PAMELA** *romantic music.**)

(**PAMELA** *appears. Engrossed in a light novella.* **HANNAY** *entranced. He marches in, sweeps her into his arms.*)

HANNAY. Darling! How lovely to see you!

(*They kiss passionately. She shrieks. Slaps him hard.*)

Listen I'm so terribly sorry I really am! But I was desperate! My name's Richard Hannay. They're after me for murder. I swear I'm innocent! You've got to help me! I've got to keep free for the next few days. The safety of this country and the whole world depends upon it –

(*The door opens. Two* **POLICEMEN** *appear.*)

POLICEMAN 1. Sorry to disturb you sir, madam. But might either of ye seen this man passing in the last few minutes? His name is Richard Hannay and he's extremely dangerous.

PAMELA. This is the man you want Inspector! He pushed in here and forced himself upon me. He told me his name was Richard Hannay!

POLICEMAN 2. Is your name Richard Hannay?

HANNAY. Certainly not!

POLICEMAN 1. But this innocent young lady clearly stated –

---

* A license to produce THE 39 STEPS, EVEN MORE ABRIDGED does not include a performance license for any third-party or copyrighted music. Licensees should create an original composition or use music in the public domain. For further information, please see Music Use Note on page 3.

(**HANNAY** *pushes open the door. He leaps out and clings to the side of the train.*)

Oh my God sir! We're on the –

(Looks down. Gasps!)

Agggh!!! Forth Bridge sir!

POLICEMAN 2. I can see that, constable! After him man!

(**POLICEMAN 1** *leaps out of the train after* **HANNAY.**)

(Sound effects: Train roars into black tunnel. Train piercing whistle.)

Highland Train. Ext. Night.

(**HANNAY** *appears on the train roof. Coat flapping.* **POLICEMAN 1** *follows him. Cape flapping.* **POLICEMAN 2** *and* **PAMELA**'s *heads out of the window.*)

POLICEMAN 2. Don't look miss! Grab him man!

POLICEMAN 1. Very good sir yes sir.

PAMELA. Might I make a suggestion? Why not –

POLICEMAN 2. Little bit busy miss.

(**POLICEMAN 1** *keeps chasing, lunges at* **HANNAY.** *Misses.*)

POLICEMAN 1. Missed him sir!!!

POLICEMAN 2. Missed him miss.

PAMELA. – Just pull the communication cord!

POLICEMAN 2. No miss! Whatever you do! Do not pull the –

(**PAMELA** *pulls the cord. The brakes slam on. The train screeches to a halt.* **HANNAY** *and* **POLICEMAN 1** *crash forward.* **PAMELA** *screams. Smoke fills the stage.*)

(*Sound effects: Train screeches furiously, judders to halt.*)

(**POLICEMAN 1** *and* 2 *and* **PAMELA** *appear through the clearing smoke. They look down.*)

He's gone sir!

PAMELA. Gone?

POLICEMAN 1. To his doom madam! And good riddance to a villain!

PAMELA. Yes! Good riddance – to a villain!

> *(They all laugh happily.* **PAMELA** *not quite so sure.)*

> *(Fade to black.)*

> *(Sound effects: The buzz of a plane fades up. The plane louder, circles round.)*

> *(***HANNAY** *appears, bedraggled, soaked, dirt on face.)*

> *(Sound effects: Plane louder.)*

> *(***HANNAY** *crawls desperately.)*

> *(Sound effects: Machine gun fire.)*

> *(***HANNAY** *ducks and dives.)*

> *(Sound effects: Bullets strafe the ground around him.)*

> *(***HANNAY** *runs, dodging the bullets.)*

> *(Sound effects: The plane louder and louder. It screeches and dives.)*

> *(***HANNAY** *runs, rolls, dives for his life.)*

> *(Sound effects: Plane explodes!)*

> *(Burning light & smoke.)*

> *(The smoke clears.* **HANNAY** *looks up.)*

Alt-Na-Shellach. Front Door. Night.

(A grand front door. ALT NA SHELLACH above it. **HANNAY** *stumbles towards it. Pulls doorbell.)*

(Sound effects: Avon chimes: Ding dong!)

(The door opens. An aristocratic lady in tweeds – **LOUISA JORDAN**.*)*

MRS JORDAN. Yes?

HANNAY. I am so sorry to disturb you. I am looking for Professor Jordan. It's really quite important.

MRS JORDAN. I am the Professor's wife. Louisa Jordan. May I know your name?

HANNAY. My name is – Hammond. Tell him a friend of – Miss Annabella Schmidt.

MRS JORDAN. Miss Annabella Schmidt? Do come in if you would please Mr Hammond.

(She swings the door round. **HANNAY** *steps through. He is now inside.)*

Alt-Na-Shellach. Corridors. Night.

MRS JORDAN. Follow me please.

HANNAY. Thank you.

MRS JORDAN. Not that way. This way.

HANNAY. Sorry.

Alt-Na-Shellack: Professor's Study. Night.

MRS JORDAN. Ah! Here we are. My husband's study. Wait here if you would please. I'll fetch him directly.

(She exits. **PROFESSOR JORDAN** *appears at speed in his armchair.)*

PROFESSOR. Mr Hammond! So sorry to have kept you.

HANNAY. It's quite alright.

PROFESSOR. So – you're from Annabella Schmidt?

HANNAY. She's been murdered you know!

PROFESSOR. Murdered!!? How dreadful!

HANNAY. And now the police are after me!

PROFESSOR. I'll get rid of them don't you worry Mr – Hannay. I suppose it's safe to call you by your real name now?

HANNAY. Quite safe.

PROFESSOR. But listen. Why did you come all the way to Scotland to tell me about it?

HANNAY. Because I believe Annabella was trying to tell you about some secret top secret air ministry secret secret and she was killed by a foreign secret agent who's after it too. She was looking for something called – ah yes! The Thirty-Nine Steps!

PROFESSOR. The Thirty-Nine Steps?

HANNAY. If we can find out what the Thirty-Nine Steps are then –

PROFESSOR. So – tell me Mr Hannay – did she happen to tell you what this foreign agent looked like?

HANNAY. There wasn't time. Ah yes! Wait! There was one thing. Part of his little finger was missing.

(Holds up a little finger.)

This little finger I think.

PROFESSOR. Are you sure it wasn't –

(Pause: Holds up stump.)

– this one? *(He holds up his own little finger. It is cut off at the knuckle.)*

HANNAY. I'm not sure I think -

(Sees the stump. Gasps! The **PROFESSOR** *pulls out a revolver.)*

PROFESSOR. Mr Hannay. I'm afraid you've forced me into a very difficult position. You see I live here as a respectable citizen. My very best friend is the Sheriff of the County. So my whole existence would be ruined if it "came out" that I was not "what I seem". But what makes it doubly important that I simply cannot let you go is that I'm about to convey some very vital information out of the country. Oh yes! I've got it alright. I'm afraid poor Annabella Schmidt would have been far too late. In her great mission to save humanity! Her beloved people!

(Laughs.)

Ha ha ha! So I'm afraid there is only one option, Mr Hannay.

(Aims revolver at **HANNAY.***)*

Unless of course you care – to join us.

(Lowers revolver.)

HANNAY. Join you?

PROFESSOR. When the var comes.

HANNAY. Var?

PROFESSOR. The greatest var there vill ever be.

HANNAY. *(Gasps, he realises the* **PROFESSOR** *is German.)*

PROFESSOR. Even greater than the Great Var. But this time – we shall be the Wictors! That's why we need YOU Hannay. You have the exact qualities we require. Absolute ruthlessness. Unmitigated unscrupulousness. Inhuman intelligence. Utter heartlessness. A man in other word, mit no mercy, no conscience. Oh yes. We know you very well Mr Hannay! Or may call you Rickard? Such a sad story. So terribly sad. No-one to love. No little home of your own. No little schnucki wooki to share it with! So terribly lost aren't you old chum!?! But you don't need to be you see! There is a home. And many many to share it with! The home – or heim – of the Master Race! Commanded eternally by destiny itself! Well!? Will you join us? Rickard!!??

(Pause. **HANNAY** *thinks.)*

HANNAY. Alright Professor! If you think I'm suitable material.

PROFESSOR. Oh yes! YES YES YES! I do I do old sport! How unutterably wunderbar!

(Calls out.)

Mrs Jordan! Mrs Jordan!

HANNAY. Oh and sorry! Just one thing. One last little tiny question. Before I – sign up.

PROFESSOR. Of course! Anything! Anything!

HANNAY. What exactly are – the Thirty-Nine Steps?

PROFESSOR. The Thirty-Nine Steps! Though I say so meinself – is my own brilliant idea!!! The very soul of the enterprise! The cream on the strudel!

(Stops! Gasps!)

But wait a minute!! Wait a MINUTE! You thought you could join us and SPY!?? You're as bad as she was mit all her outmoded save the world sentimental highminded bovenscheissedrivel. You thought you could pull ze wool!!?

HANNAY. Master Race? I despise you!

(*The* PROFESSOR *clutches his heart.*)

PROFESSOR. Ach! Achh! No no no no!! Ha ha ha! The Thirty-Nine Steps!!!? You will never ever EVER KNOW!

(*He aims revolver.* MRS JORDAN *enters.*)

MUSIC: OFF-STAGE – ["WAGNER THE RIDE OF THE VALKYRIES"]

MRS JORDAN. You called dear?

PROFESSOR. Just to say, my dear, Mr Hannay will not be joining us for lunch.

(PROFESSOR *aims.*)

MRS JORDAN. What a shame. Goodbye Mr Hannay.

HANNAY. NOT SO FAST PROFESSOR!!!!!!

(HANNAY *dives.* PROFESSOR *shoots.*)

(*Blackout.*)

MUSIC: ["WAGNER THE RIDE OF THE VALKYRIES"] – very loud

(*Sound Effects: Gunshots. Screams. Breaking glass.*)

MUSIC: ["WAGNER THE RIDE OF THE VALKYRIES"] – climaxes and cuts

Sheriff's Office. Night.

(The **SHERIFF** *at his desk. Laughing loudly. A phone with handle on the desk. A man with his back to us.)*

SHERIFF. Thank God thank God you're here sir! And there was me thinking he was my friend! Calling himself a professor! Whereas all along he was –

(The man turns. It is **HANNAY.** *Worse for wear but still in one piece.)*

HANNAY. A spy!

SHERIFF. A spy!

(Winds phone handle.)

Hello?

(Turns to Hannay.)

Tea Mr Hannay?

HANNAY. No tea for me, thank you. Now look here sheriff –

SHERIFF. Biscuit?

HANNAY. No biscuit thank you! This is serious you know!

SHERIFF. Quite right quite right.

(Sotto into phone.)

Whenever you're ready inspector?

HANNAY. Otherwise I'd hardly put myself in your hands with a murder charge hanging over me?

SHERIFF. Ach! Never heed the murder Mr Hannay! Just need a quick statement to forward to the proper authorities.

(On phone.)

Quickly man!!

HANNAY. Statement!? There's no time for a statement! The professor's got the information don't you see?! And it's absolutely vital to the safety of our air defense –

(INSPECTOR *bursts in.*)

INSPECTOR. You wanted to see me sheriff?

SHERIFF. Yes and about time Inspector! Do you think I enjoy playing for time with a *MURDERER!!!*

HANNAY. *MURDERER???*

SHERIFF & INSPECTOR. *MURDERER!!!*

SHERIFF. Richard Charles Arbuthnot Hannay? You are under arrest! On the charge of the wilful murder of Annabella Schmidt in Portland Mansions, Portland Place London on Tuesday last. Handcuffs Inspector!

INSPECTOR. Yessir! C'm 'ere you!

(INSPECTOR *pulls out handcuffs. Tries to force them on to* HANNAY's *wrist.*)

HANNAY. But you heard my story! It's true!

SHERIFF. I don't believe any of your cock-and-bull story! Professor Jordan is my personal friend and in my personal opinion the most personable Englishman in all of Scotland! Hurry with the handcuffs Inspector!

INSPECTOR. *(Wrestling.)* Yes sir! Right away sir!

SHERIFF. *(Turns handle.)* Get me Professor Jordan this moment!

HANNAY. Professor Jordan!!!???

SHERIFF. Yes indeed the very self-same Professor Jordan who you accuse of treason!? You're in deep water Hannay and it's getting deepier by the second!

(Turns handle.)

Yes! Get me professor – No! No tea thank you!

HANNAY. Now listen here! I demand that you allow me to speak to the Foreign Office in London!

SHERIFF & INSPECTOR. Foreign Office in London! Ooooo!

*(We hear a **LITTLE VOICE**.)*

LITTLE VOICE. Hello! Hello!? Hello!?

*(They all stop. Listen for the **VOICE**. Realise it's coming from the phone. **SHERIFF** grabs the phone.)*

SHERIFF. Hello? Hello?? Professor!!?? Professor!!??

(Winds handle.)

Professor!!! PROFESSOR!!!!????

*(To **INSPECTOR**.)*

HANDCUFFS MAN!

INSPECTOR. *(Grabs **HANNAY**, clicks on cuff.)* First cuff on now sir!

LITTLE VOICE. Hello! Hello!?

SHERIFF. *(Winds handle.)* Hello!? Hello!? Ahhhh! Professor Jordan! Thank God sir! God bless you sir! Yes indeedy this is the Sheriff sir! Just to say sir we have apprehended the villain sir! Everything is hunky dory and fully tickety – tickety –

(He looks at the phone.)

Ach! Professor? Professor Jordan!!?

(Winds handle.)

Get me Professor Jordan this moment please!

(Winds handle.)

Now ye listen here ye – CRETIN!!! Ye bletherin – bletherin – ach Professor! Professor! So terribly sorry sir!

(Falls to his knees, hyperventilating.)

So terribly terribly humbly sorry sir! Everything's fine and dandy sir thank ye sir! Utterly hunky dory and tickety – tickety – OTHER HANDCUFF INSPECTOR!!!

INSPECTOR. Right you are sir! OTHER CUFF SIR! GOIN ON NOW SIR!!!

*(The **INSPECTOR** leaps on to **HANNAY**.)*

HANNAY. OH NO YOU DON'T!!!

*(**HANNAY** knocks the **INSPECTOR** to the floor. He leaps out of the window.)*

(Sound Effects: Smashing glass.)

(He runs off-stage, trailing a handcuff, straddling the window.)

INSPECTOR. He's leapt from the window sir! Stop that man!

*(The **INSPECTOR** charges after him.)*

SHERIFF. As I was saying sir? Ha ha ha! Everything's fine sir! Everything – hunky – er – dory and hunkily – tickety – wickety – boo sir – um –

(Makes guttural noises to make phone sound like bad line.)

– rather a bad line sir! It's the weather sir. The Highland storms – coming up the airy mountain, down the rushy – rushy – glen sir!

(Guttural noises build.)

(Sound effects: Police bells and whistles.)

(Chase music louder & louder.*)

---

* A license to produce THE 39 STEPS, EVEN MORE ABRIDGED does not include a performance license for any third-party or copyrighted music. Licensees should create an original composition or use music in the public domain. For further information, please see Music Use Note on page 3.

Scottish Streets. Night.

(**HANNAY** *running through the dark streets. Searchlights and torches pursue him. Realises he is cornered. Suddenly:*)

(*The skirling pipes and drums of a Scottish marching band.*)

(*The* **TWO MEN** *enter as the Regiment of the Royal Argyll and Sutherland Highlanders.* **HANNAY** *takes his chance. He nips in and marches with them. They exit marching.*)

Assembly Hall. Night.

(A banner across the back of the stage: VOTE McCORQUODALE. A very old man **MR DUNWOODY** *enters with a chair.* **HANNAY** *bursts in.)*

HANNAY. Excuse me! Sorry sorry! Can you possibly help me?

DUNWOODY. Why! Helloo! Hellooo! Ye're here at last!

HANNAY. Am I?

DUNWOODY. He's here Mr McQuarrie!

(An even older old man appears. **MR MCQUARRIE.** *Dragging a lectern.)*

MCQUARRIE. He's here! He's here! Thank the Lord! Thank the Lord!

(The old men grab **HANNAY,** *plonk him in the chair, straighten his tie.* **DUNWOODY** *stands at the lectern.)*

(Sound effects: Applause.)

DUNWOODY. Thankee thankee! And without further ado Mr McQuarrie will now introduce this evening's special guest speaker! Mr McQuarrie if you would please?

*(***MCQUARRIE** *hobbles toward the lectern. He begins his speech of welcome. He is entirely inaudible.)*

MR MCQUARRIE. Well ladies and gentlemen there's no need for me to tell you of our special guest speaker's –

DUNWOODY. Mr McQuarrie sir? Speak up sir.

MCQUARRIE. Speak up?

DUNWOODY. Speak up. Ay.

MCQUARRIE. Right ye are.

(Even less audibly.)

– many and remarkable qualities. His brilliant record as soldier, statesman and poet speak louder than words. Which is more than can be said for me.

(He laughs uproariously.)

He is here tonight to urge you most emphatically to return our candidate Mr McCorquodale by an overwhelming majority. So a big welcome please for guest speaker – Captain Rob Roy McAlistair!

(Sound effects: Applause.)

*(**HANNAY** sits there smiling. Looks round for Captain McAlistair. Realises they mean him. Looks aghast. Marches to the lectern.)*

HANNAY. Ah right, well ladies and gentlemen I must apologise for my slight hesitation in addressing you just now but to tell you the simple truth, I'd entirely failed while listening to the chairman's flattering description, to realise he was talking about – me.

(Sound effects: Roars of laughter.)

Thank you so much! Anyway as I – journeyed up to Scotland on the Highland Express over that magnificent structure the Forth Bridge I had no idea I'd shortly be addressing such an historic gathering.

(Accidentally reveals handcuff. The two old men notice. They look worried.)

Anyway – may I say right away how truly relieved I am to find myself in your presence at this moment –

*(**PAMELA** enters.)*

Oh hello! Do take a seat. Just about to get to the best –

(They gaze at each other.)

(Romantic music.*)

Good heavens! Hello!

PAMELA. Hello!

(She snaps out of it. Runs out.)

(Romantic music: Cuts.)

HANNAY. Anyway we're all here tonight to discuss – what shall we discuss? I know! How about the idle rich? Not that I can talk about that because I'm not rich and I've never been idle.

(Sound effects: Laughter.)

Thanks awfully. Actually I've been pretty busy most of my life really. Well actually not recently. Recently I've been in a bit of a slump. Well not that recently. Recently, the last few days, well the last *day* really –

*(**PAMELA** re-enters. Whispers urgently to the old men.)*

– everything's gone a bit haywire frankly. Pretty damn bonkers if you want to know. But the odd thing is – *the odd thing is* – you carry on!

*(**PAMELA** and the men exit hurriedly. **HANNAY** carries on regardless.)*

---

* A license to produce THE 39 STEPS, EVEN MORE ABRIDGED does not include a performance license for any third-party or copyrighted music. Licensees should create an original composition or use music in the public domain. For further information, please see Music Use Note on page 3.

HANNAY. And it's pretty – bracing when you do! You're just thinking of jacking it all in when – I don't know – something gets the old ticker pumping again. And there's no time to think. And your mind's singing. And your heart's racing. And you've never felt like this before. And you realise something you've never realised. That the world's not so bad and the people in the world, they're not so bad either! And we shouldn't be thinking of ourselves all the time! And fighting our corner, but thinking of them! Thinking of other people too. All the – what does it say on the Statue of Liberty? The tired, the poor –

> (**PAMELA** *re-enters with the two* **HEAVIES.** **HANNAY** *keeps going, playing for time.*)

HANNAY. – the homeless, the tempest-tossed, the yearning to breathe free!

> **MUSIC:** Charles Hubert Hastings Parry's **["JERUSALEM"]** – Fades up to rousing crescendo

Because we should be looking after each other! Not fighting each other! Saving the world not destroying it. Is that such an outmoded sentimental notion? A world with no persecution or hunting down! Where suspicion and cruelty and fear are forever banished! That's the sort of world I want! Is that the sort of world you want? Come on! Let's vote on it! I'm asking you.

> (*Points at members of the audience.*)

You. You. And you too! And definitely *you!* Come on! Vote yes! For a new world! A free world! A better world! And above all for –

> (*Looks up at the banner.*)

– Mr McCrocodile!! Thank you.

(Sound effects: Applause.)

MUSIC: Charles Hubert Hastings Parry's ["JERUSALEM"] – Climaxes

PAMELA. This is the man you want Inspector!

HANNAY. Where have I heard those words before?

*(He makes a bolt for it. The **HEAVIES** grab him. Snap the handcuff on his other wrist.)*

HEAVY 1. That'll be all miss, thank you, you've been most helpful. Come along now sir.

HANNAY. Now look here! There's an enormously important secret being taken out of this country by a devilishly brilliant foreign agent! I can't do anything myself because of these fool detectives! But if you telephone Scotland Yard immediately –

PAMELA. I'll do no such thing! Goodbye Mr Hannay.

HANNAY. Just telephone Scotland Yard and –

HEAVY 2. Actually beg pardon miss – er –

PAMELA. Edwards. Pamela Edwards.

HEAVY 1. – on second thoughts, Miss Edwards, we should like you to come too.

PAMELA. Me? But you just said –

HEAVY 1. Just to the police station miss.

HEAVY 2. If you wouldn't mind miss. Just to Inveraray miss.

PAMELA. *INVERARAY!!??* But that's nearly –

HANNAY. Forty miles miss.

PAMELA. *FORTY MILES!!??*

HEAVY 1. You keep out of this!

HEAVY 2. He's to be questioned by the Procurator Fiscal personally.

PAMELA. Procurator Fiscal personally?

HEAVY 2. It's essential for public security miss.

PAMELA. Essential for public security? Well I suppose if it's absolutely necessary!

HEAVY 2. Thank you miss. Much appreciated miss. If you'd just like to pop into the car miss?

(HANNAY *and* PAMELA *look for the car.*)

PAMELA. Pop into the what!?

HEAVY 1. Car miss.

PAMELA. What car?

(HANNAY *sighs. The men grab chairs. Make the car.* HEAVY 1 *sits in the front. A steering wheel thrown on.* HEAVY 1 *turns the key.*)

(*Sound effects: Motorcar noises.*)

(HEAVY 2 *helps* PAMELA *into the back seat. Pushes* HANNAY *beside her. Climbs in next to* HEAVY 1.)

HANNAY. Ah hello!

PAMELA. I'm not talking to you.

HANNAY. Right.

(HANNAY *whistles the* MR MEMORY *tune.*)

Police Car. Night.

(Driving music.*)

(Sound effects: Car roars, tyres screech.)

*(They lurch and skid along the winding roads. **PAMELA** starts.)*

PAMELA. Wait a minute! This is the wrong road! This is the road south. Inverary's north surely.

HEAVY 2. There's a bridge fallen down on that road Miss. We shall have to go round. The man knows the way Miss.

HANNAY. Would you have a small bet with me Pamela?

*(**PAMELA** scowls.)*

Alright I'll have it with you Sherlock. I'll lay you a hundred to one that your Procurator Fiscal has the top joint of his little finger missing.

*(**HEAVY 1** whacks **HANNAY**. He grins.)*

I win.

(Sound effects: Car brakes screech.)

(Car lurches to a stop.)

---

* A license to produce THE 39 STEPS, EVEN MORE ABRIDGED does not include a performance license for any third-party or copyrighted music. Licensees should create an original composition or use music in the public domain. For further information, please see Music Use Note on page 3.

The Open Moor. Night.

PAMELA. Now where are we?

(Sound effects: Bleating sheep sounds.)

HEAVY 2. Damned sheep! We'll have to clear them away! Come along man!

HEAVY 1. What do we do wi' him?

HEAVY 2. Here's what we do wi' him!

(Grabs HANNAY's handcuff. Unlocks it, snaps it on to PAMELA.)

PAMELA. What are you doing! Unchain this handcuff!

HEAVY 2. Now you're a special constable miss. As long as you stay – he stays! Come on! Oota the way ye bleating brutes!

(The HEAVIES exit chasing sheep.)

HANNAY. And as long as I go – you go. *COME ON!*

(Jumps out of the car. Pulls her after him.)

(Sound effects: POLICE whistles.)

PAMELA. Police! POLICE!!! Help! Help! *HEEEELP!!!*

HANNAY. Right. Feel this – pistol?

(Sticks his pipe in her back.)

Want me to shoot you stone dead?

PAMELA. Not particularly no.

HANNAY. Then get a move on!

PAMELA. Help!!! Help!!!

HANNAY. Listen! One more peep out of you, I'll shoot you first and myself after. I mean it! Now come along!

(He yanks her. She sinks.)

(Sound effects: Squelch!)

PAMELA. I'm stuck in a bog! I can't move!

HANNAY. Yes you can. Come on!

*(**HANNAY** pulls her.)*

(Sound effects: Squelch!)

PAMELA. Ow!

*(**HANNAY** marches on, pulls her after him. He whistles.)*

Look you can't possibly escape you know! What chance have you got, tied to me?

HANNAY. I'd keep that question for your husband if I were you.

PAMELA. I don't have a husband!

HANNAY. Lucky him! Come along!

(He whistles chirpily.)

PAMELA. Will you please stop whistling!

HANNAY. Oh look!

PAMELA. What?

HANNAY. A river!

(Calling into the wings.)

A river!!

(The men leap on with a blue cloth that they ripple across the stage.)

(Sound effects: Roaring river.)

PAMELA. *(Recoils in horror.)* I am not crossing that!

HANNAY. Breast stroke? Or a lazy crawl?

(He wades in, she pulls back.)

(Sound effects: River roars louder.)

PAMELA. I can't – actually – um –

HANNAY. What?

PAMELA. – swim!

HANNAY. Oh marvelous. Twenty million women on this island and I have to be chained to you! Right come on!

(He picks her up in his arms.)

PAMELA. Stop that! What are you doing? Take me back this moment! Do you hear me?

HANNAY. No turning back now! Sorry!

(He wades on. The men hold the rippling cloth higher.)

PAMELA. PUT ME DOWN!! HOW DARE YOU!! PUT ME DOWN THIS MOMENT!

HANNAY. Alright in that case I'll put you down and you'll sink like a stone. And you'll drag me with you. What's it to be? Live together? Or die together?

(The men hold the cloth up to HANNAY and PAMELA's necks.)

PAMELA. Stop it! Stop it! Don't be ridiculous!

(To the men.)

Put it down! PUT IT DOWN!! STUPID BOYS!!

(The men sheepishly lower the cloth. **HANNAY** *plonks her on the other side.)*

HANNAY. Right. On we go. Come on!

*(**HANNAY** marches off. Pulls her after him. Whistling chirpily.)*

PAMELA. Will you stop whistling!

HANNAY. What IS that tune!?

PAMELA. Listen, Richard Hannay, wanted man, those policemen will get you just as soon as it's light. You know that, don't you?

HANNAY. Listen, Pamela whatever your name is –

PAMELA. Edwards.

HANNAY. Edwards. You don't know Schnozzle Edwards?

PAMELA. NO!!!

HANNAY. Funny you look just like him! Those policemen are not policemen and I'll say this one more time. There's a dangerous conspiracy against this country and we're the only people who can stop it!

PAMELA. Same silly penny novelette spy story!?

HANNAY. Alright then! If you prefer you're alone on a dark moor, manacled to a murderer who'll stop at nothing to get you off his hands! Is that better?

PAMELA. I'm not afraid of you!

(Sound effects: Thunder. Sudden downpour.)

Oh no!!!!

(Sneezes.)

HANNAY. Bless you.

PAMELA. Thank you.

(She looks at him. He looks at her. A tender moment. He drags her on.)

HANNAY. Now come on!

(Sound effects: Thunder.)

PAMELA. OW!!! You just don't care do you!? All you care about is your selfish, pompous, beastly, horrible, horrid, heartless heartless heartless –

VOICE (MRS MCGARRIGLE). Hellooooo!

HANNAY. Wait a minute! What's that?

VOICE (MRS MCGARRIGLE). Hellooooo! Hellooooo!

(Neon 'HOTEL' sign comes into view.)

HANNAY. Look! It's a – it is! A little tiny Highland hotel! And look! A little tiny Highland hotel landlady!

*(**MRS MCGARRIGLE** trots out.)*

MRS MCGARRIGLE. Ach! I thought I heard something! Ye poor wee dears! Come in, come in and welcome to the McGarrigle Hotel!

McGarrigle Hotel. Reception. Night.

MUSIC: ["SCOTTISH MUZAK"]*

(HANNAY and PAMELA enter MR MCGARRIGLE behind the reception desk. Keys, guest book, phone.)

MRS MCGARRIGLE. Now then, I am Mrs McGarrigle. This is my husband Willie McGarrigle.

MR MCGARRIGLE. Aye!

HANNAY. Hello!

MR MCGARRIGLE. Aye!

HANNAY. Say hello darling.

MR MCGARRIGLE. Hello darling

MRS MCGARRIGLE. Not you Willie! Silly Willie! Oh! Just one thing. We just have the one room left I'm afraid. With the – er – one bed in it. Ye are man and wife I suppose?

PAMELA. Um –

MRS MCGARRIGLE. What is it my dear? Is anything wrong?

HANNAY. No no there's nothing wrong. She wants to tell you something that's all, don't you darling? The thing is we're – a runaway couple.

MRS MCGARRIGLE. Ach I thought ye were! Well your secret's safe wi' us. Willie!

MR MCGARRIGLE. Aye!!

---

* A license to produce THE 39 STEPS, EVEN MORE ABRIDGED does not include a performance license for any third-party or copyrighted music. Licensees should create an original composition or use music in the public domain. For further information, please see Music Use Note on page 3.

HANNAY. Well thanks awfully! Isn't that super darling?

(*Nudges* **PAMELA**.)

Darling!

PAMELA. Super!

MRS MCGARRIGLE. Ach! Tender young love! I'll just away tae light a fire in your room.

(**MRS M** *exits, returns instantly.*)

There we are! A fine roaring fire awaits ye! Come away the noo!

HANNAY. The what?

MR MCGARRIGLE. The noo.

HANNAY. Right. Come along my darling. Away the – noo.

(**MRS MCG** *heads off.* **HANNAY** *pushes* **PAMELA** *after her.* **MR MCG** *follows.*)

MRS MCGARRIGLE. Just doon here. Round the corner. Up the stairs. Mind your wee heads. Down two more steps. Along the corridor. And here we are. The bridal suite!

(*They open door. Reveal a fireplace, a big double bed.*)

McGarrigle Hotel. Bedroom. Night.

MRS MCGARRIGLE. Lovely soft bed. Fine roaring fire.

> *(They all turn to the fire. Nothing happens. They all wait. It bursts into flame.)*

And we'll bid ye both a very good "first night".

> *(Giggles.)*

If ye follow my drift.

> *(Smitten.)*

Ah the wee young doves! Willie!

MR MCGARRIGLE. *(Smitten too.)* Aye?

MRS MCGARRIGLE. *OOT!!!*

MR MCGARRIGLE. *OOT!!!*

> *(**MR MCG** exits. **MRS MCG** follows.)*

PAMELA. Now look here! If you think I'm going to spend the whole night alone with you in this – this –

> *(Sneezes.)*

Achooo!

HANNAY. Listen you better get that damp skirt off.

PAMELA. I shall keep it on thank you!

> *(Shivers.)*

Actually, I will take my shoes off. And my – stockings.

> *(She turns and awkwardly removes her stockings.)*

HANNAY. Can I be of assistance?

PAMELA. No thank you!

(**HANNAY** *looks steadfastly away.*)

HANNAY. Warmer now?

PAMELA. Yes thanks.

HANNAY. Jolly good.

(*He leads her to the bed. She starts to follow.*)

PAMELA. *WAIT A MINUTE! What are you doing!!?* I am not lying on that bed!

HANNAY. It's the only bed there is I'm afraid. Sorry.

> (**HANNAY** *climbs on to the bed. She climbs miserably after him. He starts whistling.*)

PAMELA. *Will you please stop whistling!*

HANNAY. I wish I could get that damn tune out of my head.

(*Yawns loudly.*)

D'you know when I last slept in a bed? Saturday night. Whenever that was. Then I only got a couple of hours.

PAMELA. What woke you? Dreams? I imagine murderers have terrible dreams.

HANNAY. Dreadful yes. Ever since I started out on my life of crime. I never had a chance you see. Poor little orphan boy. That was me my darling. Irredeemable. Irreclaimable. Utterly horrid and beastly and what was it?

PAMELA. Heartless.

HANNAY. Exactly. I'd get away from me as quick as you can if I were you! Oh no, you can't, can you? Are you sure you don't know Schnozzle? Oh well...

> (**HANNAY** *snores loudly. She gazes at him tenderly. Pulls herself together. Twists off the*

handcuff. Jumps out of bed. Puts her hand in his pocket. Finds the pipe. Sees it's not a pistol, slams it on the mantelpiece. Exits.)

McGarrigle Hotel. Reception. Night.

(The two **HEAVIES** *at the desk. One talks urgently into the phone. The other leans in, listening.)*

HEAVY 2. Mrs Jordan! Listen please! Mrs Jordan!

*(***PAMELA** *appears, listening.)*

We *had* to take the girl as well as Hannay!

*(***PAMELA** *gasps!)*

No Mrs Jordan! We lost 'em on the moor! It was the sheep you see! He'll have told her the whole plot by now! She'll know we're not the real police!

*(***PAMELA** *aghast!)*

What's'at Mrs J? Dispose of 'em? As soon as we find 'em? Yes madam! Just as you say Madam! We'll ditch em – in a ditch! Beg pardon madam? He's what? Has he? Is he? Does he? Very good madam! Good thinking madam! Goodbye madam!

(Slams down receiver.)

Guess what? The professor's got the wind up and he's clearin out! Says it's too dangerous with Hannay and the girl on the loose. He's warning the whole Thirty-Nine Steps!!

HEAVY 1. The whole Thirty-Nine Steps!!? Blimey!! Does he have the – you know?

HEAVY 2. Certainly does! He's picking up our friend from the London Palladium tonight on the way out. We gotta get to the Professor! Pronto!

(They jam on their trilbies. Run out, bump into each other, exit.)

(Sound effects: Car starts. Roars away.)

McGarrigle Hotel. Bedroom. Dawn.

(Sound effects: Morning birdsong.)

(PAMELA walks in. Gazes down at HANNAY.)

PAMELA. Morning!

HANNAY. *(Wakes with a start. Sees the empty handcuff.)* What are you doing!? Wait a minute! How did you get out of these? Why didn't you run away?

PAMELA. I did. Then, just as I was going, I discovered you'd been speaking the truth. So I thought I'd stay. So look here! Those two policemen came here last night. They're not policemen!

HANNAY. I *KNOW* they're not policemen! I *said* they weren't policemen!

PAMELA. Sorry.

HANNAY. So what did they say?

PAMELA. Oh – um – yes! A lot of stuff about – something with a number. Twenty – thirty... Thirty! Thirty –

HANNAY. Nine!

PAMELA. Thirty-*Nine!* That's right. Thirty – nine –

HANNAY. Steps!!!

PAMELA. *Thirty-Nine Steps!* Exactly! How did you know that? Anyway someone's going to warn them! How can you warn steps?

HANNAY. Never mind!! Go on!!

PAMELA. Right! And yes! Someone's got the wind up and is clearing out. And – they're picking someone up from the London Palladium.

HANNAY. London Palladium? London Palladium? Who's that I wonder. Is that the Professor? Our friend with the little finger missing? What's he want to go there for? Funny thing for a master-spy to do!

PAMELA. I feel an awful fool for not having believed you.

HANNAY. That's alright.

> (*He sits on the bed. They gaze at each other with sudden tenderness.*)

> (*Romantic music.**)

Well – I suppose – we – ought to be – um…

PAMELA. Yes?

HANNAY. …going really.

> (*Neither moves.*)

Which um…

PAMELA. What?

HANNAY. …room are they er staying in?

PAMELA. Who?

HANNAY. Those two men.

PAMELA. Staying in?

HANNAY. Mmm.

> (*They are very close.*)

PAMELA. Well they're not.

HANNAY. What?

---

* A license to produce THE 39 STEPS, EVEN MORE ABRIDGED does not include a performance license for any third-party or copyrighted music. Licensees should create an original composition or use music in the public domain. For further information, please see Music Use Note on page 3.

PAMELA. They went away as soon as they'd telephoned. They drove off into the night. Rather fast actually.

HANNAY. *(About to kiss her.)* Where?

PAMELA. Don't know. Sorry.

> *(Waiting for the kiss.)*

Does it matter?

> *(HANNAY leaps up.)*

HANNAY. *DOES IT MATTER!!!???*

> *(Music cuts out.)*

PAMELA. *What!!?*

HANNAY. *WHY DIDN'T YOU STOP THEM!!!???*

PAMELA. Who!?

HANNAY. The two men!!! Why didn't you stop them!?

PAMELA. Because I wanted to see you!!

HANNAY. Well that was a stupid thing to do wasn't it!!!

PAMELA. Apparently yes!!!

HANNAY. So where did they go?

PAMELA. I don't know! The London Palladium I suppose!!

HANNAY. The London Palladium!!? When!!?

PAMELA. Tonight! On the way out!

HANNAY. *ON THE WAY OUT!!?? ON THE WAY OUT OF WHAT?*

PAMELA. *I DON'T KNOW WHAT!!!*

HANNAY. Well that's four or five precious hours wasted!

PAMELA. Well if they're all leaving the country that's fine isn't it? Just leave well alone!

HANNAY. *Leave well alone!?* I am accused of murder! The only way to clear my name is to expose these spies!

PAMELA. *Your* name! *YOUR* name! You see! All you think about is your *SELF!* Your horrible beastly horrid selfish pompous horrible heartless heartless –

HANNAY. But *MUCH* more important than *CLEARING MY NAME!* Is that they are about to leave the country with a secret vital to the safety of our country! *VITAL TO THE SAFETY AND SECURITY OF THE WHOLE WORLD!!!!*

PAMELA. WELL I'M VERY VERY VERY SORRY!!!

HANNAY. WHICH SHOW MATINEE OR EVENING!!!

PAMELA. I DON'T KNOW!!!

HANNAY. WELL THANKS FOR YOUR HELP! GOODBYE!!!

PAMELA. GOODBYE!!! AND DON'T EXPECT ME TO COME WITH YOU!!!

HANNAY. I WON'T!!!

PAMELA. GOOD!!!

HANNAY. GOOD!!!

PAMELA. I'M NOT SURPRISED YOU'RE AN ORPHAN!

> (**HANNAY** *storms out. Slams the door.* **PAMELA** *bursts into tears.*)

The Road to London. Night.

(Lights up on **HANNAY**. *Motoring goggles. Driving furiously.)*

(Sound effects: Screeching tyres.)

Telephone Box. Night.

PAMELA. Hello yes. Scotland Yard? It's about Richard Hannay. The man wanted for murder! Except he didn't. No. What!? Because I – listen! I need to speak to the Chief Commissioner please! It's Pamela Edwards here and it's a matter of life and death actually! And what? Oh hello? Uncle Bob is that you? Thank God! Fine thanks! Now look, about Richard Hannay! He's gone to the – is it okay to tell you? Okay sorry Uncle Bob. To the – London Palladium!

> **MUSIC: ["LONDON PALLADIUM THEME SONG"]***

---

* A license to produce THE 39 STEPS, EVEN MORE ABRIDGED does not include a performance license for any third-party or copyrighted music. Licensees should create an original composition or use music in the public domain. For further information, please see Music Use Note on page 3.

London Palladium. Stage. Night.

RECORDED VOICE. This is the London Palladium!

> (**HANNAY** *appears in a theatre box. Staring through binoculars.* **PAMELA** *appears behind him.*)

PAMELA. Hello.

> (**HANNAY** *is delighted but acts cross.*)

HANNAY. What on earth are you doing here?

PAMELA. I'll go then shall I?

HANNAY. Er no – you'd better stay now you're here.

PAMELA. Righto.

HANNAY. But now look here! I've found him!

PAMELA. Who?

HANNAY. The Professor.

PAMELA. With the little finger missing?

HANNAY. Yes!

PAMELA. Which little finger?

HANNAY. It doesn't matter which little finger! He's over there! In the box. There! D'you see?

> (*A hand holding opera glasses appears in the opposite box.*)

PAMELA. Gosh yes! But there's nothing you can do! I've talked to Scotland Yard.

HANNAY. Scotland Yard!!!?

PAMELA. My uncle's Chief Commissioner actually. Uncle Bob.

HANNAY. Bob?

PAMELA. Yes.

HANNAY. Bob's your uncle?

PAMELA. Yes. And nothing's been stolen from the Air Ministry. Nothing. No secret top secret information or anything even remotely secret.

HANNAY. But those men said the professor's got it!

(*Looks at the audience and gasps!*)

MY GOD!! POLICE! What are they doing here? You didn't tell them I was here did you?

PAMELA. Oh dear! Sorry!

HANNAY. Well that's it then. That's IT!!!!!

MUSIC: ["MR MEMORY THEME"]

(**COMPERE** *enters.*)

(*Sound effects: Applause.*)

COMPERE. And now a big warm welcome please for one of the most remarkable men ever in the whole world. Mr Memory.

(*Enter* **MR MEMORY.**)

HANNAY. Wait a minute! That's the damn tune I couldn't get out of my head!

(**COMPERE** *exits.*)

MEMORY. Thankoo ladies and gentlemen. I will now make myself ready and prepared for this evenin's performance.

MUSIC: ["DRUMROLL"]

(**MEMORY** *looks up at the* **PROFESSOR**'*s box. The* **PROFESSOR** *signals to* **MEMORY.**

> MEMORY *nods to the* PROFESSOR.
> PROFESSOR *disappears.)*

HANNAY. I've got it! I'VE GOT IT! Of course they don't think anything's missing! All the information's in Memory's head! That's why the Professor's here tonight. To take Memory out of the country. With the information!

MEMORY. First question please! How high is the dome of St. Paul's Cathedral? The Dome is precisely two hundred and seventy –

> *(*SUPERINTENDANT ALBRIGHT *enters.)*

ALBRIGHT. Richard Charles Arbuthnot Hannay?

HANNAY. Yes?

ALBRIGHT. Detective Chief Superintendant Albright sir. Scotland Yard sir. I am arresting you on a charge of MURDER!

> *(Sound effects: Audience gasp!)*

HANNAY & PAMELA. *MURDER!?*

PAMELA. But he's innocent I tell you Chief Detective Chief Inspector Superintendant Detective Albright!

HANNAY. Alright alright Albright. I'm sorry Pamela there's – no other way.

> *(Nips behind curtain.)*

ALBRIGHT. Very wise sir. Now if you'd – *(notices)* Hang on! He's escaped!! QUICK!! Block all the exits!! Carry on as normal Mr Memory please.

> *(*ALBRIGHT *rushes out.)*

MEMORY. Very good sir, thank you sir. As I was sayin. The height of St Paul's Cathedral is two hundred and –

(**HANNAY** *swings in on a rope.*)

HANNAY. *WHAT ARE THE THIRTY-NINE STEPS?*

(**MEMORY** *freezes.*)

I SAID WHAT ARE THE THIRTY-NINE STEPS!!? Come on man! Answer up!

(**MEMORY** *freezes. Looks wildly between the* **PROFESSOR** *and* **HANNAY.***)*

MEMORY. Thirty-Nine Steps sir? Thirty-Nine Steps?

HANNAY. Yes Mr Memory! For the last time! *WHAT ARE THE –*

MEMORY. *(Into automatic.)* The Thirty-Nine Steps is an organisation of spies. They collect information on behalf of the Secret Service of – the Secret Service of –

(*The* **PROFESSOR** *appears with a revolver. Shoots* **MEMORY.***)*

(*Sound effects: Gunshot. Audience panic.*)

(**MEMORY** *sinks to the ground.*)

HANNAY. There! That's the man you want Detective Chief Inspector Superintendant Albright!!

PROFESSOR. Too late Hannay! This is not your story. No no no! This is *my* story! And I decide how it ends. You don't destroy me Hannay! And you don't get the girl!

(*He swings the revolver at* **PAMELA.***)*

(**PAMELA** *screams.*)

HANNAY. Down Pamela! Get down!

PROFESSOR. No no no you don't Hannay! You lose the girl and you die of grief! That's how your story ends. You thought you found true love? Afraid not old sport! You

never will you see. You will die, as you lived, unloved
and all alone in your dull little rented Portland Place
flat! A lost man. Forever lost. Such a sad story. So
terribly terribly sad. Goodbye my dear young lady. I'm
so sorry it had to end like this. Who knows? You and I,
we might have –

> (*He aims at* **PAMELA**. *She braces herself
> bravely. Suddenly* **HANNAY** *is in the box
> beside him* **HANNAY***is in the box.*)

HANNAY. I don't think so Professor!

> (**HANNAY** *grabs the* **PROFESSOR**. *They
> wrestle, appearing and disappearing.*)

> (*A gunshot.*)

> (*The* **PROFESSOR** *appears. But not the real*
> **PROFESSOR**. *A* **DUMMY PROFESSOR**. *The*
> **DUMMY** *falls into the audience.*)

> (*Sound effects: Audience panic.*)

> (**MR MEMORY** *staggers up.*)

MR MEMORY. Don't panic! Don't panic ladies and gents!
Stay calm! Stay calm! Bring on – the dancing girls!

MUSIC: ["DANCING GIRLS MUSIC"]*

> (**MEMORY** *collapses.*)

---

* A license to produce THE 39 STEPS, EVEN MORE ABRIDGED does
not include a performance license for any third-party or copyrighted
music. Licensees should create an original composition or use music in
the public domain. For further information, please see Music Use Note
on page 3.

London Palladium. Backstage. Night.

(**HANNAY** *and* **PAMELA** *run on with the* **COMPERE**. **MEMORY** *is dying.*)

HANNAY. Mr Memory? What was the secret formula you were taking out of the country?

MEMORY. The biggest job I ever had to tackle! Is it okay for me to tell you sir?

HANNAY. Of course it is old man.

MEMORY. *(Fast and without a pause)* The first feature of the new engine is its greatly increased ratio of compression, represented by r minus one over r to the power of gamma and nine, sequenced to the power of xy forty-nine squared and duplicated notwithstanding by thirty-two point, seventy-one point and eighty-eight point recurrin', aligned to eleven double governor valves flowing –

(*He slumps. They bow. He wakes.*)

– radially in series with longitudinal pressure exerted on the turbine shafts and counterbalanced by a twelve point nine grooved piston at an angle of point sixty-seven omicron recurrin'. This device renders the engine – completely – silent. Am I right sir?

HANNAY. Quite right old chap.

MEMORY. Glad it's off my mind at last sir.

(**MR MEMORY** *dies.*)

(*Sound effects: Dancing girls fade/busy 30s London Street.*)

Oxford Street, Outside Palladium. Night.

(**HANNAY** *and* **PAMELA** *enter.*)

HANNAY. Well –

PAMELA. Well done.

HANNAY. Well done you.

PAMELA. You're a free man anyway.

HANNAY. Right.

PAMELA. Saved the world too.

HANNAY. We both did that.

PAMELA. I hardly –

HANNAY. Damn well did!

PAMELA. Well I –

(*They look at each other. A moment.*)

HANNAY. Anyway – better be – you know –

PAMELA. Right.

HANNAY. Got the decorators in and – you know –

PAMELA. Yes.

HANNAY. Anyway. Bye.

PAMELA. Bye.

HANNAY. Bye.

(*They exit in opposite directions.*)

Hannay's Flat. Night.

(*Enter* **HANNAY**. *Looks round the room, pulls the dust-sheet off the table. Lifts the phone. Listens. Puts it back. Opens the blind. Pulls it down fast. Freezes.*)

(*Effects: Distant front door opens. Footsteps come upstairs. Closer and closer. Closer and closer. Closer and closer. They reach his door. They stop.*)

(*Nothing happens.* **HANNAY** *grabs the handle. Pulls open the door.*)

HANNAY. RIGHT! Now look here –

(*There is* **PAMELA**.)

PAMELA. I've been thinking.

HANNAY. I have also.

PAMELA. What about?

HANNAY. The most beautiful girl I ever saw on a train. Who I can't stop thinking about. What have you been thinking about?

PAMELA. A poor little orphan boy who never had a chance. I can't stop thinking about him either.

(*She marches up to him.*)

HANNAY. Um – little difficult with the – you know – decorators and –

PAMELA. This is the man I want Inspector.

(*Puts her arms round him. They stand in each other's arms.*)

HANNAY. What's that – um – drumming noise?

PAMELA. I think it's our hearts.

HANNAY. So shall we er –

PAMELA. Probably.

HANNAY. Right.

> *(They are about to kiss. They've been here before.)*

DISTANT: ["HARK THE HERALD"]

Is it Christmas?

PAMELA. Christmas Eve actually.

HANNAY. So it is. Good Lord. Happy Christmas Pamela Edwards.

PAMELA. Happy Christmas Richard Hannay.

> *(They kiss.)*

> *(A little Christmas tree rolls on.)*

HANNAY. Can I call you Schnozzle?

PAMELA. No.

HANNAY. Right.

> *(They kiss again.)*

> *(The little tree lights up.)*

> *(The **TWO MEN** appear in the window. Smiling and scattering snow.)*

MUSIC: ['BUILDS TO CLIMAX"]

The End

ABOUT THE AUTHOR

PATRICK BARLOW is probably best known for his role as Desmond "Olivier" Dingle the Artistic Director and Chief Executive. Together with John Ramm as Raymond Box, they are the renowned two-man National Theatre of Brent, which Patrick created in 1980. The NTOB has become something of a legend in British theatre, television and radio. Their abbreviated comedy epics include: *The Charge of the Light Brigade, Zulu!!, The Black Hole of Calcutta, Gôtterdämmeriing Wagner's Ring Cycle* (in an hour and a quarter), *Greatest Story Ever Told, Love Upon the Throne* (the Charles and Diana story) which was nominated for an Olivier Award, *The Messiah, The Wonder of Sex, Massive Landmarks of the Twentieth Century* for Channel 4 and their many acclaimed Radio series include: *The Arts and How They Was Done, All the World's a Globe, Iconic Icons, Giant Ladies That Changed The World, The First Man on the Moon* and *How They Done It* for BBC Radio 4. They have won two Sony Gold awards, a Premier Ondas Award for Best European Comedy and a New York Festival Gold Award for Best Comedy. Patrick's other screenwriting includes: *The Growing Pains of Adrian Mole, The True Story of Christopher Columbus, Queen of the East, Van Gogh* (Prix Futura, Silver Bear Berlin Film Festival), *Revolution!!* (Best Comedy Jerusalem Film Festival), the BAFTA-winning *Young Visiters* and *Why Didn't They Ask Evans?* for the Miss Marple series and ITV Other Stage Writing includes: *A Christmas Carol* (nominated for an Olivier Award) starring Jim Broadbent as Scrooge, an adaptation of Milton's *Comus* for the Sam Wanamaker Playhouse at Shakespeare's Globe, *Ben Hur – Tale of The Christ, The Six Wives and Reg* for Hampton Court. For Radio: *Joan Of Arc and How She Finally Became a Saint* starring Dawn French and *Starchild* for BBC Radio 4, Patrick's publications include: *Shakespeare – the Truth!* and *All The Worlds A Globe – from Lemur to Cosmonaut – An Inexhaustible History of the Whole World.* Patrick's Screen and Theatre acting credits include: *Shakespeare in Love, Notting Hill, The Diary of Bridget Jones, Nanny McPhee, Absolutely Fabulous, Jam & Jerusalem, Miranda, Is It Legal?, A Very English Scandal, Why Didn't They Ask Evans?* adapted by Hugh Laurie. *Loot, A Funny Thing Happened on the Way to the Forum and 'Toad'* in Alan Bennett's *Wind In the Willows.*

The 39 Steps was a hit show with 139 characters played by four actors. It has been performed in over 40 countries worldwide and ran for nine years at the Criterion Theatre in the West End. *The 39 Steps* won Patrick an Olivier Award for Best Comedy, a WhatsOnStage Award for Best New Comedy in the UK and

Helpmann and Molière Awards in Australia and France for Best Play. His Broadway adaptation co-won the Drama Desk Award for Unique Theatrical Experience and was nominated for four Tony Awards including for Best Play and won two Tony Awards for Best Sound Design and Best Lighting Design. In 2010 *The 39 Steps* held a record as the longest running Broadway play in seven years having played 771 performances.

When the show finally closed in The West End, the London run had recorded the fifth-highest number of performances of any West End play. During the course of its run our Producers, Edward Snape and Marilyn Eardley, claimed they got through "3,000 pairs of stockings, 530 maps of Scotland, 38 pairs of handcuffs and 16 suspender belts".

It's estimated that 3 million people have seen a version of *The 39 Steps* worldwide.